Joe Camp's Benji™

Benji's Big Adventure

By Scout Driggs & Joe Camp

Photos by Tony Demin

Based on the screenplay by Joe Camp

HarperKidsEntertainment

An Imprint of HarperCollins*Publishers*

This is Benji.

Benji is a very smart dog.

He has an important mission.

This is Lizard Tongue.

Lizard Tongue is a very silly dog.

His mission is to have fun,

get plenty to eat,

and drive dogcatchers crazy!

The story of Benji and Lizard Tongue

is quite an adventure!

Benji has an important job to do.

He needs to save his mother, Daisy.

She is very sick.

Daisy's owner, Mr. Hatchett,

is not a nice man.

He keeps Daisy outside in the cold,

locked in a dirty cage.

Benji has a plan to rescue Daisy

before things get any worse.

To save his mom, Benji has to learn how
to open the latch on her cage.
He watches Mr. Hatchett through a hole
in the fence.

Now all Benji has to do

is find the right time.

Finally, Mr. Hatchett is gone.

The yard is empty.

The right time is now!

Benji is ready to rescue Daisy.

He slowly creeps toward the cage.

But wait . . .

Here comes Lizard Tongue!

He is running fast.

He is barking like crazy.

People are chasing Lizard Tongue!

Oh, no—

the dogcatchers!

Lizard Tongue is in big trouble.

Benji will be in big trouble, too,

if he does not get away!

But Benji has to save Daisy.

What should he do?

If Benji gets caught,

he will not be able to save his mother.

So he follows Lizard Tongue

into the woods.

The dogcatchers are right on their tails, but the two dogs outrun them.

Whew!

That was close.

Lizard Tongue and Benji are out of trouble for the moment.

Now Benji must save Daisy.

He will do it alone because Lizard Tongue

is on the run from the dogcatchers.

So Benji sneaks into Mr. Hatchett's yard.

He stands on his hind legs
to see into Daisy's cage.
Daisy does not look well.

Benji carefully lifts the latch,

just the way

he saw Mr. Hatchett do it.

It works!

The cage door swings open.

Benji helps his mother out of the cage.

Quickly, they leave the yard.

Benji takes Daisy to an old, empty house.

Daisy can hide there.

She will be safe.

But Daisy is so sick she cannot even eat
the turkey leg Benji found for her.
She needs a doctor.

How can Benji get Daisy to a doctor?

He has an idea—the dogcatchers!

They will bring Daisy to a doctor!

For that, Benji needs Lizard Tongue's help.

Lizard Tongue's job is to lead

the dogcatchers to the old house.

They are always chasing him anyway,

so it should be easy.

After all, the dogcatchers are not

mean like Mr. Hatchett.

They like to help dogs.

They can help Daisy.

Lizard Tongue and Benji

find the dogcatchers.

"Warf!" Lizard Tongue says.

The dogcatchers see Lizard Tongue and

the chase is on.

Lizard Tongue and Benji run straight for the old house.

The dogcatchers follow the two dogs all the way there.

When the dogcatchers enter the house,
they see Daisy.

They can tell right away that
she needs help.